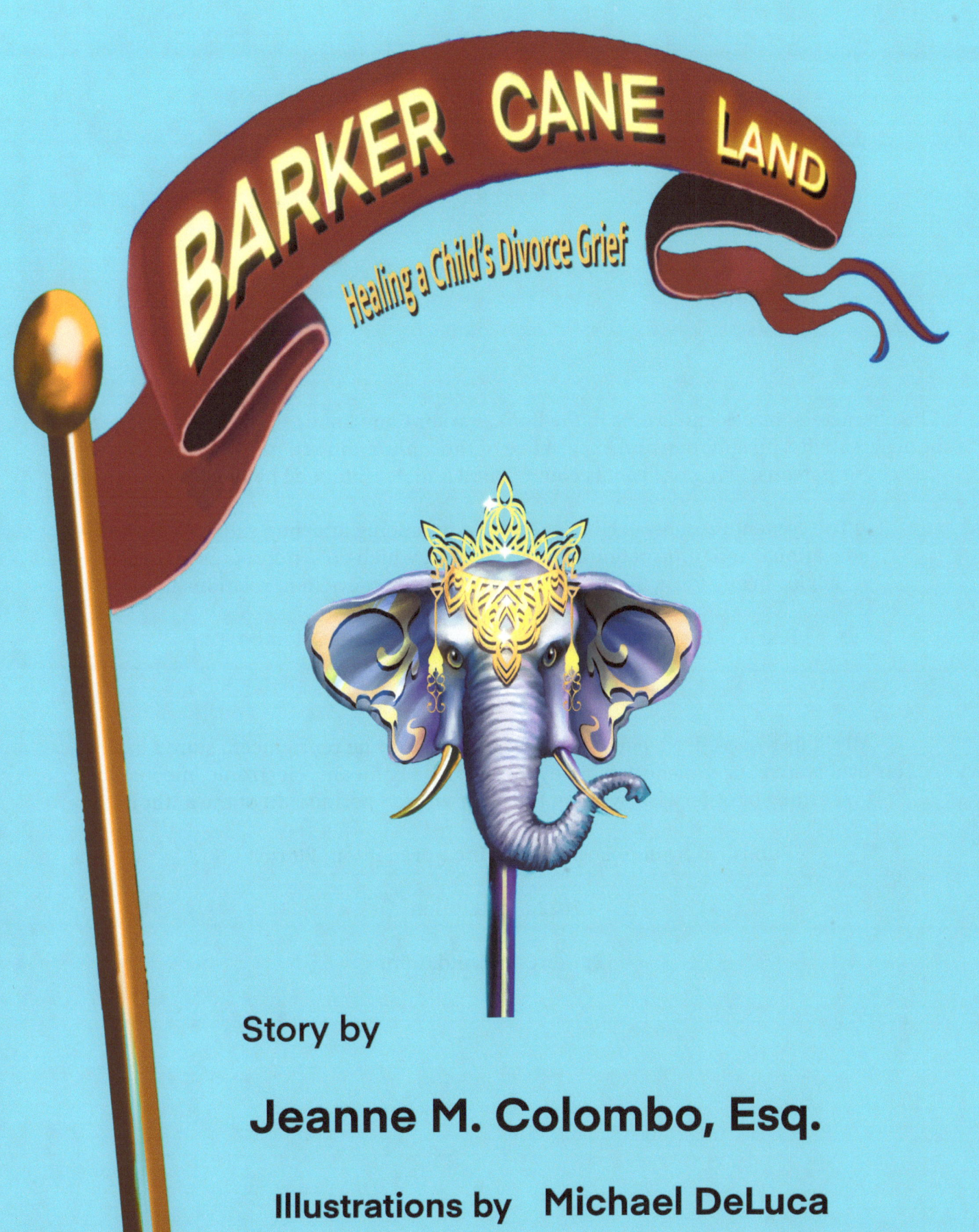

BARKER CANE LAND
Healing a Child's Divorce Grief

Story by

Jeanne M. Colombo, Esq.

Illustrations by   Michael DeLuca

The characters, places and events in the book, Barker Cane Land, are fictitious, the product of the creativity, imagination and experience of the author and artist. Any similarity to real places or persons, living or dead, is coincidental and not intended by the author or artist.

The content presents original views of a practicing attorney, intended for educational and informational purposes only, which does not represent legal advice in any form, and does not create an attorney/client relationship.

Text and Images Copyright © 2022 by Jeanne M. Colombo, Esq.

ISBN 978-1-64719-902-9

All rights reserved. No part of this publication may be reproduced, stored in a retrieval system, or transmitted in any form or by any means, electronic, mechanical, recording or otherwise, without the prior written permission of the author.

Published by BookLocker.com, Inc., Bradenton, Florida USA.

2022 First Edition

BarkerCaneLand.Com

Dedicated to all of my North Stars, especially you, Jan.

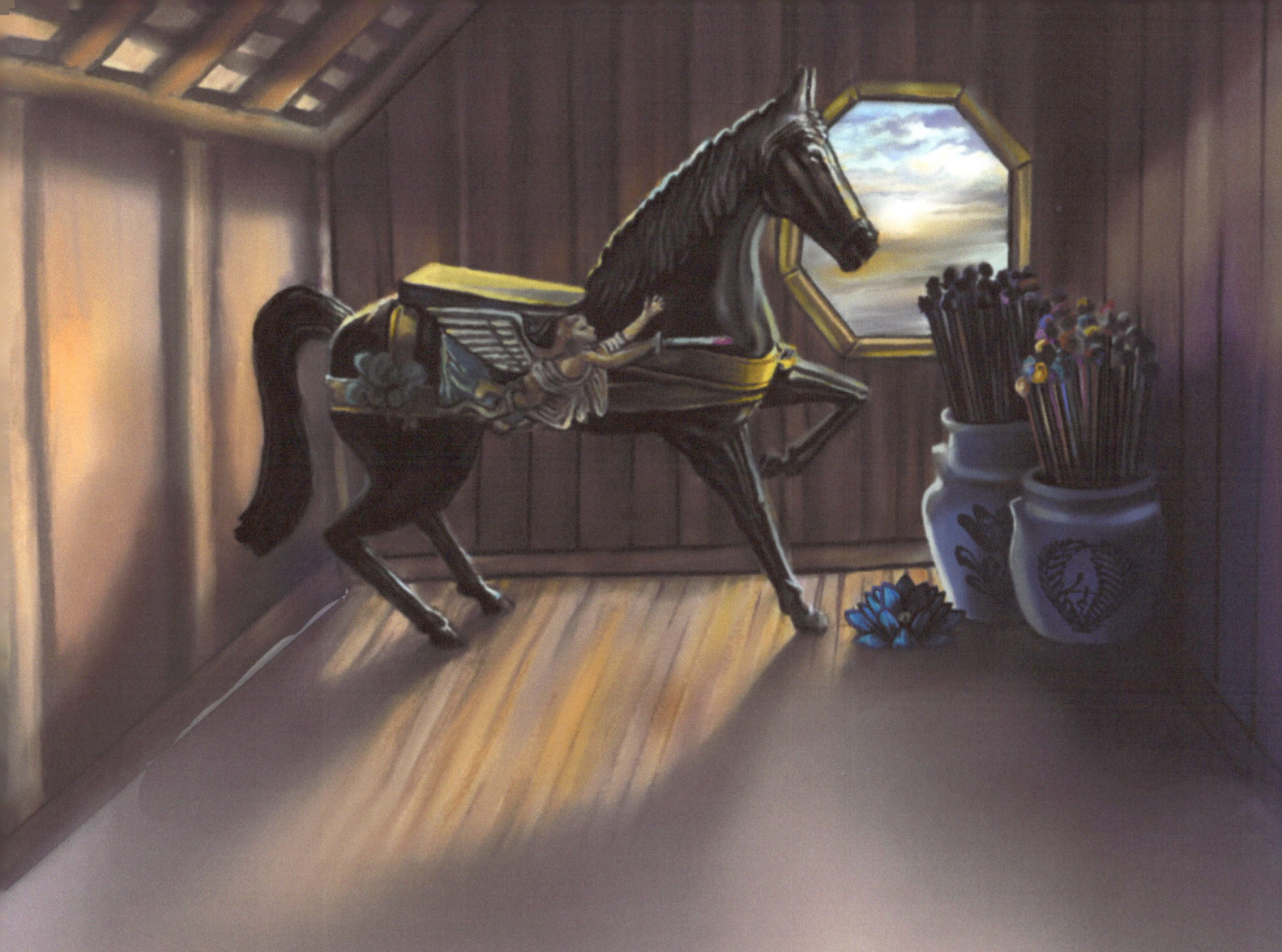

Chapter One: Grandma's Attic

"I just want this Grief and Sadness of my Parents' Divorce to Stop!"

A sad Young Lad begs as he enters his Grandma's dusty old attic, tears in his eyes. His hand is on his heart. He says to himself, but out loud, *"No one hears your voice when you are young. My parents are just not listening…"*

He gets his bearings in the darkened attic space, and goes over and looks at an old Carousel Horse that is in a corner, lit by an outside window. He notices the wooden horse has an avenging angel on its side. *"Hmm,"* he thinks to himself, *"to protect."* Not knowing what to do with all of his conflicted emotions, he begins to dust the neglected horse off with love, tenderness and care. As he does so, he thinks to himself, *"How can my parents be splitting up? How do I get this heartbreak to end? It actually physically hurts. I don't know how I can bear all of this. My world is crashing."*

The Young Lad still can hear his parents downstairs at his Grandma's kitchen table telling him, and his twin sister, that they cannot do it anymore; they are divorcing. He can still see his sister's eyes filling with tears. He shakes his head, and just sobs. With much effort, he continues to focus on his task of cleaning the neglected and dusty horse, in an effort to forget his loneliness, when the horse starts to shimmer and shine, and *"What? Is it? Can it be? Alive? Has the horse moved?"* the Young Lad marvels. *"Is that a glimmer in the horse's eye?"*

The Young Lad's affection has freed the Carousel Horse, and she whinnies with joy and wild abandon.

The Young Lad cannot help himself and jumps onto the Horse's saddle. And that is when he notices the Barker Canes in Grandma's old butter crocks. One crock is decorated with the blue laurel victory wreath, that reminds him of a courageous champion from history class.

All of a sudden, he remembers his Grandma's delight in telling him what fun she had collecting the Barker Canes as prizes at the old traveling carnival fairs, when she was a young girl. And here they all were together, as if they were waiting for something, or someone.

He looks closer. He sees the Canes are porcelain heads of different animals and objects, with tassels, on long wooden sticks. One Barker Cane seems to move ever so slightly. *"Did I really see that?"* the Lad quizzically wonders to himself. The Cane seems to be beckoning to the Young Lad. The Horse leans forward towards the Barker Canes.

The almost imperceptible movement of the Barker Cane is enough to make the boy grab for the Cane, an Elephant.

As he holds the smooth band of the long cane, he too is rendered 'magical'. His plea brings the magic of the Canes to the fore. Whoosh, Magic, Lights, Rainbow Colors, and Fireworks illuminate the air and walls in the attic.

Out of the antique stoneware crocks, the porcelain Barker Canes all rise. They dance and hover in the air. They all look alive!

The Young Lad can barely hold on to the Carousel Horse and the Elephant Cane. He closes his eyes to concentrate…Time seems to speed up, then slow. The Young Lad is on a dizzying ride of his life.

Chapter Two: The Midway

Boom! All of a sudden...all stop!

He knows he is finally safe. He opens one hazel eye with golden flecks, then the other.

He rubs his eyes, as he lets go of the Elephant Cane, which rises in the air. He is at a traveling carnival fair in the year 1946!

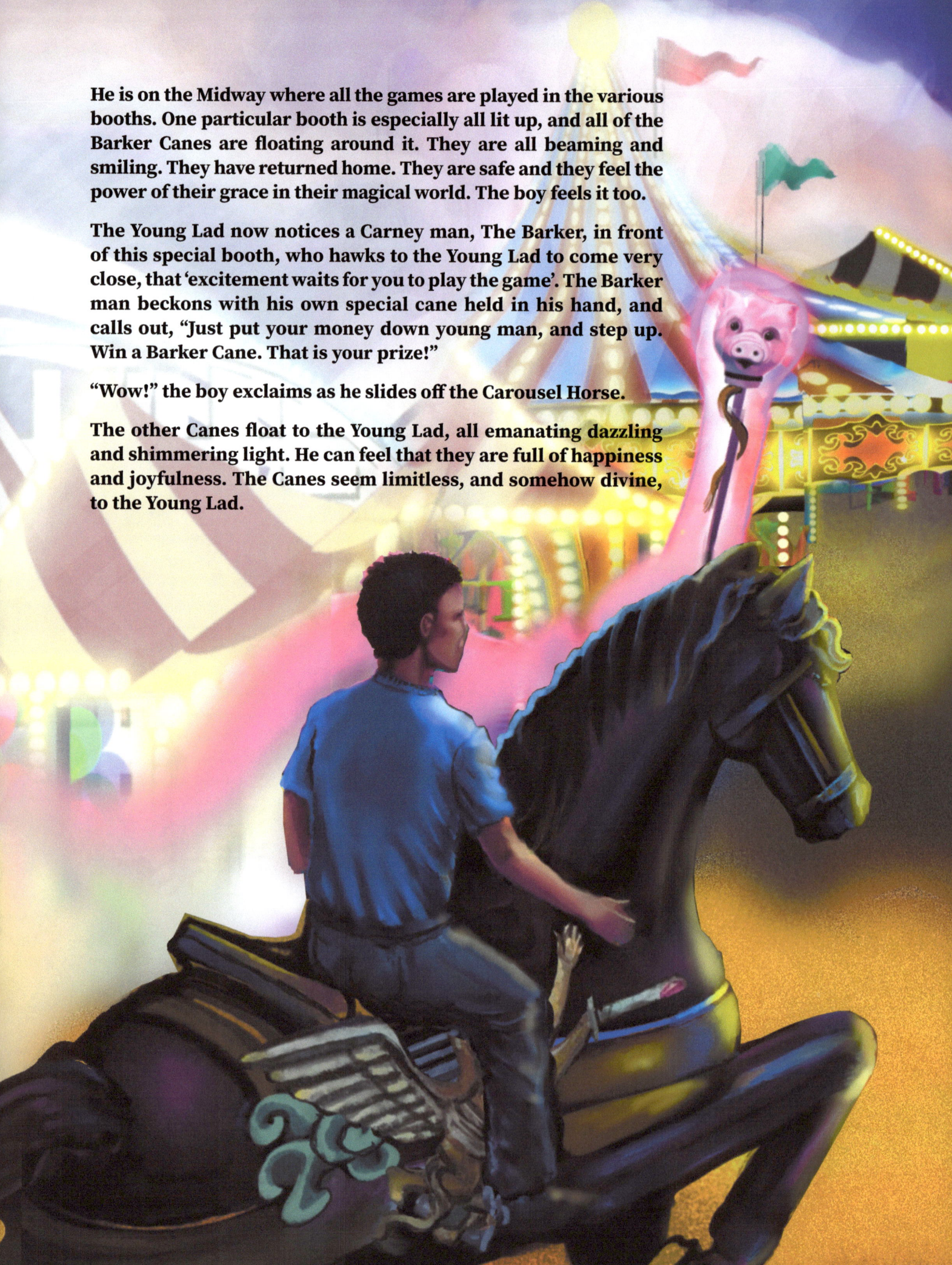

He is on the Midway where all the games are played in the various booths. One particular booth is especially all lit up, and all of the Barker Canes are floating around it. They are all beaming and smiling. They have returned home. They are safe and they feel the power of their grace in their magical world. The boy feels it too.

The Young Lad now notices a Carney man, The Barker, in front of this special booth, who hawks to the Young Lad to come very close, that 'excitement waits for you to play the game'. The Barker man beckons with his own special cane held in his hand, and calls out, "Just put your money down young man, and step up. Win a Barker Cane. That is your prize!"

"Wow!" the boy exclaims as he slides off the Carousel Horse.

The other Canes float to the Young Lad, all emanating dazzling and shimmering light. He can feel that they are full of happiness and joyfulness. The Canes seem limitless, and somehow divine, to the Young Lad.

The Elephant Cane, not yet in his full grandeur, moves over to the Young Lad and says, "Indeed, admission here is by invitation only. The Grand Presence, at you service," and the Cane 'bows' a welcoming.

The boy starts to beam, and stating, and questioning, at the same time, "You are alive? For real?"

The Elephant Cane turns to the Young Lad, and thunderously proclaims, "I am the Remover of Obstacles. With the flow of grace, you call it magic, you can unravel this creature called Grief that has landed in your heart, because of the misplaced actions of your parents towards each other. I tell you, while they never meant to unleash this very real creature called Grief on you, they did. Their act of physically leaving each other, it must be understood, made the Grief truly happen. It is like it splattered all over you. It is now yours, but we Barker Canes will help you sort it all out. We promise."

So, as the Barker man said, "Step up, aim well, throw the ball, and hit your mark. The prize will be in your grasp, be revealed, and then will be yours to take home."

The Young Lad softly takes the ball. He tosses it up and down in his hand, getting the feel of it. He is thinking about his conflicted feelings. He takes a deep breath, steadies himself, focuses on the hole in the booth wall, and drills the ball into the bull's eye. He lets out a satisfied shout, "Yes!" and relaxes just a bit.

Chapter Three: The Dog Cane

His first prize floats to him. It is a Dog Cane!

The Dog Cane licks the Young Lad's cheek. The Young Lad can't help himself, and laughs, something he has not done in quite a while. The Dog Cane barks, "May I introduce myself; I am called Allegiance. Consider me your game changer to this sport called Grief. Take hold of my collar," he commands the Young Lad. "I am unconditional devotion and affection, and I will not let you drop the ball."

The Dog Cane wolfs, "Make no mistake, I am absolutely, forever loyal to you. It is in my very nature," as he shakes his Cane, as if he had a tail. "I hear you. I see you. I know you. I support you. To gain victory over this painful sport, keep that understanding in your Heart Center. When you start to stumble in your daily living, remember I am your loyal friend, and recall your friend's words for you to be comforted."

"We Barker Canes are each unique, but we are always a family. And always will be forever your family. We are devoted to you. Thus, we will always be within your grasp. As with us, so with your loved ones. While, right now, it may appear otherwise, that family bond can never be broken between you and your parents. Take comfort in that knowledge."

"You see, you are my most worthy companion. Yes, you indeed are absolutely worthwhile," the Dog Cane howls. "And that self-worth, my friend, has power that will help connect you to those you hold most dear. Because whether you want to admit it or not, those dear ones are your parents."

"We Barker Canes sparkle in all directions because of the unity of the Light that is inside of, guess who?" He points. "You!"

"So, know your journey is to be kind to yourself, seek harmony, find the wonder, have courage. Be happy and joyful. Listen to the wisdom that the Barker Canes bestow on you! Hear us in your Heart."

Chapter Four: The Horse Cane

At that moment, there is a Horse Cane that glides to the Midway Booth and faces the Young Lad. Her beautiful mane is flowing in the air. Allegiance says, "Let me introduce you to Glory. She is a most spiritual warrior, and comes just for you."

Glory rises up and whinnies, "While you now feel like a stranger in Your own story, the majesty of your path awaits you!"

"Confidence in your Self will give you freedom. Yes, it takes strength to carry you through your sadness, your anxiety, and your stress, because of how the conflicts and arguments of your parents touch you."

"Consider that no one has absolute control over another person, including you! But, you do have sole influence over your own inner self, your Heart Center. If you can just determine to make an inner shift and center yourself; you can cast out the fear and frustration of the situation."

The Young Lad gazes at Glory and questions, "How do I do that?" Glory softly nickers, "Well, to center yourself, visualize that you are a warrior whose silvery steel shield reflects the Light against the Darkness. Your center is the dancing flames of strength that shine the Light that will make the shades of Grief burn away."

"The hidden truth is you are perfect! That is your glory! There is power in finding your new story." The Horse Cane flips her mane.

"So, stay in the flow of the life force that will protect you and carry you through this life challenge. The separation of your parents is one of those challenges (the first of many) you will have to face. Welcome to life! It is a wild ride, don't you know?"

The Horse Cane charges in the air, and neighs, "So, here is an exercise to help you find that graceful flow. Close your eyes, take three fresh breaths, in and out, go slow. Breathe in deep, gently hold it, and exhale out long. Let your mind quiet as it watches and feels, your beautiful, lifegiving breath. Each molecule in your body loves the renewal of the breath. As your mind quiets with the breath, so now will your heart feel that life force coursing through every part of your body. Understand when something is right, your whole body breathes well. It lets go of the negativity, and fills itself with the blue sky of joy.

Do it as often as you need. It really works."

"Make no mistake, I tell you, You are that **POWER!** You are absolutely Amazing!"

Chapter Five: The Pig Cane

The Young Lad, who now is deeply lost in his thoughts and trying to absorb the advice of the Barker Canes, hears, "Heads up!" as a Barker's Midway ball comes hurtling at him. At the last moment, he catches the ball. The Pig Cane travels towards him. "Lots to figure out, huh? Well get ready for it, as there is an abundance of more to come."

"I am Zesty. I know stuff."

"The trouble with Grief is, it causes things like sadness, depression, darkness and fear. Grief builds barriers and separates you from your Self. I do understand!" the Pig Cane snorts.

"You have to learn to weather the storm it creates in your heart and head. It is its own creature. I may look silly, but I can show you how to get through this difficult time in your life."

"Like the Horse Cane Glory said, 'Welcome to Life.' Being a majestic being, she did not want to add what we Barker Canes know all too well: Life is Messy."

The Pig Cane chuckles, and says, "I can relate to messy. To create some order in the mess of Grief, you have to start by waking up your inner courage! Courage lets you transform. Transformation comes one small step at a time. Each step builds you up for the next step, towards hope."

"A good lesson to follow is to surround yourself with friends and family who are hopeful, fun, and full of love. No young human is an island, or all alone. Always know, you can never, ever, be abandoned. No way!"

Zesty nudges the Young Lad, "Relax. If I can be honest, remember that what is going to happen, with adults, will happen anyway. We know this, right?" The Young Lad slowly nods his head in agreement.

"Our job is to never give up. My darling little human, know that you are perfect, magnificent, and filled with splendor. That is why you may have started in that dark attic space, but you now have manifested in all of this Light, and razzle dazzle."

"This change in your life will reshape you for the good. Yes, because you have now been given the vision to see who you really are, and to know you are always surrounded by Love, whether it be us, your Barker Cane family; or who? You tell me…"

The Young Lad thought long and hard, and said," My uncle Sam, my grandma Rose, my best friend Karen, my twin Beth, and well, yes, I know, my parents too."

The Young Lad felt comforted and safe when he realized all those people really had always been there for him, had supported and protected him, and still loved him for who he was—Tryon.

Zesty smiles, nods, and snorts, "Out of the Grief, we truly learn to see. So, Young Lad, actually try it: Imagine you are breathing out the darkness of Grief, and in the Light of Love. Again, breathe out the Grief, and breathe in the Love. Your breath is the bridge to your happiness, your zest for life."

The Pig Cane squeals knowingly with pleasure, and ends his conversation with, "Mark my words, it is Your Life, Your Light. No situation, even a divorce, can take you away from your beautiful Self.

Chapter Six: The Dice Cane

The Young Lad sighs deeply, taking all those words in, pondering their meaning to his circumstances. He looks around the Midway, realizing how comfortable he now is with all these lights, smells and sounds. He glances around, and in the distance hears people laughing and enjoying the circus of it all. *"So magical,"* he realizes. *"So attainable when you are in the present moment;"* but then he starts to doubt as he worries about his future, and his place in his changing family.

All of a sudden, in a burst of light, the Dice Cane levitates into the Young Lad's view. She says pointedly to him, "Are you looking for a chance to roll the dice, or are you hoping for a sure thing by using the loaded dice?"

"What will it be? Do you want to grab the brass ring? Take a chance on the highest prize to live life to the fullest?"

"Zesty, the Pig Cane, said to you 'Life is always messy'; but don't worry, I always use the humor and laughter, my dear boy, to clean it up! Why not? What have you got to lose, but that splattered Grief all over you? Looks a bit too green for my taste."

"Ahh! I see that smile cracking your face. That is good…you are figuring this all out. Learn that the smile always works to shape hope, which shapes the future. The future is unknown, or is it?"

"I am Roma, the fortune teller! Step right up and I will gaze into my crystal ball." Roma winks at the Young Lad, and says, "It is a pretty classy sphere, if I dare say so myself. Takes after its owner, don't you think?" and laughs at herself.

The Young Lad, in spite of himself, smiles again, but more broadly, this time. He senses that smiling feels 'good', just like she said it would. He peers into Roma's world of mystery.

The fortune teller continues, "You may not believe that your family now needs you, but they do more than ever. You are unique. No one can take your place or speak with your voice. You are there to shine your light to give your parents and twin sister a chance not to lose their way."

"Let's face it, your parents lost their focus, their joint purpose. Who knows why? They probably don't. But it really doesn't matter. Those loaded dice tell me that is a done deal. But this roll of the dice, ahh, tells me it is time for them to redefine their next chapter, to find their future, their separate purposes... And you know what? That is perfectly fine for them. That is what they need to do. It is OK."

Roma hesitates, then looks deeper into the glowing crystal ball. She looks up at the Young Lad and says "If your parents can focus on being kind to each other, over being right or winning, all of you can heal. How nice...kindness."

The Young Lad scoffs and says, "They are a stubborn, hardheaded pair."

The Dice Cane nods and says "I agree, but look at it this way, Positive Thinking is Mental Magic Realized. If you can imagine it, see it, the Energy will be yours to heal. You can count on it! Your parents will slowly, but surely start to shift. It takes time. Forgiveness takes time. Which indeed is my expertise," Roma acknowledges.

"But you, my dear boy, can control your thoughts to bring about your own miraculous change, and in the end, you are only responsible for yourself, no matter what your age is. You can always make the decision to tap into your highest and best, just for you."

"Remember, you are the very best of your parents' union. In a way, you were the reason for them being together, so they could have the crowning glory of having you in their lives. How lucky and blest they are because you happened!"

"My crystal ball sees all of this clearly, and now you can too..."

Chapter Seven: The Elephant Cane

The Midway again fills with magical light and sunshine of rainbow colors. All of the other Barker Canes bow to the Elephant Cane who once more floats in front of the Young Lad, and into the center of the other Canes. However, this time the Elephant Cane comes in his full magnificence. The Grand Presence acknowledges to the Young Lad, "I am the Triple L, if you will, Living in the Light of Love. Through the Power of Choice you can create balance by making peace with the Grief of the Divorce. Kindness towards your parents will help create the harmony—the balance. Acts of kindness will let you forgive them for being human. Their lives are not always easy."

The Elephant Cane leans down and says to the Young Lad, "I will let you in on a secret, that you already know, and I give you permission to admit out loud: Parents can be clueless!" The Elephant Cane's ears flutter with merriment.

"In this situation, parents do not always get it; that it all becomes your divorce too. It just lands out of nowhere in your lap. But we know the Truth, don't we?"

The Young Lad does not want to, but he starts giggling, as he indeed, knows it is true.

The Elephant's eyes are twinkling with laughter. He says, "Wisdom is simple. Lighten up. Healing comes from being together through a difficult time. Even if 'together' is one parent at a time."

"Kindness and laughter create cups of Love. Love shows you your self-worth. Love creates your inner Power! Your Power creates Joy and Bliss, and those put you in your own sparkling, shimmering Light."

"Your Own Truth lets you plant your feet and toes, so you can balance, in the green earth, firmly strengthen your spine upwards, and reach your hands into the blue sky. It grounds you, so you can handle whatever comes your way. Actually, remember to physically try it, when times get tough. Rise up to the sky!"

The Grand Presence leans forward and blesses the Young Lad; "With great Respect for you, with great Love, with the Grace of the Light that is You, and only You, take the Light and Love forever with you."

The Elephant Cane then whispers in the Young Lad's ear knowledge for his parents to hear so they too can bridge over their separation into their own, positively transformed lives.

The Grand Presence, the most powerful of the Canes, trumpets out: "Grief pushes into your heart and pushes your You out. You have to make the choice to come back, directly and centered, into your own heart. Only You can make the concerted effort to push Grief, and its pain, out of its comfortable spot in your heart. Only You can take back the Light. Love will flow where there is space for it.

Then you can help make that space in your family's heart. If a human listens with that healed Heart, then you can truly hear. Your parents have to learn to Hear with the Heart. While you are not ever responsible for your parents' choices, let your Light so shine that it may help illuminate their way. Then, whatever the message is will not get lost. Healing will flow amongst all of the Hearts.

For a family is a string of hearts, and you are forever connected by those hearts. It does not matter where those hearts physically live, the string is always present. If you are present, so are they.

In joy and harmony, we are miraculously free!"

Chapter Eight: Return to Grandma's Attic

The Elephant Cane, The Grand Presence, bows in honor to Tryon, and taps the Cane into the Lad's opening Heart, and Whoosh, Magic, Lights, Rainbow Colors, and Fireworks once again illuminate the air and walls in Grandma's attic…

The Young Lad, while whirling in all the dazzling light and colors, realizes that he is the writer of his own story. That he gets to walk in his own protective presence. He realizes the attic is taking shape again. The room turns slowly, almost imperceptibly, around him. He knows he has created a sanctuary in his own surroundings.

All is back in place. All is well.

The Young Lad is still on the saddle of the Carousel Horse. He has the Elephant Cane in his hand, which he carefully and lovingly places back in the crock with the other Barker Canes. He bows to them, then straightens up, very tall, heading very assuredly to the door of the attic. The Young Lad goes down to the kitchen table where his parents, sister and grandmother are sitting…

He knows that he can start to show his family how to act with divine love for each family member. *"Won't be easy,"* he thinks, *"but nothing worthwhile ever is."* He can see the Barker Canes dancing in the Flow of Love. Tryon smiles…

CPSIA information can be obtained
at www.ICGtesting.com
Printed in the USA
BVHW090442130622
639254BV00002B/24